Patricia M. Page

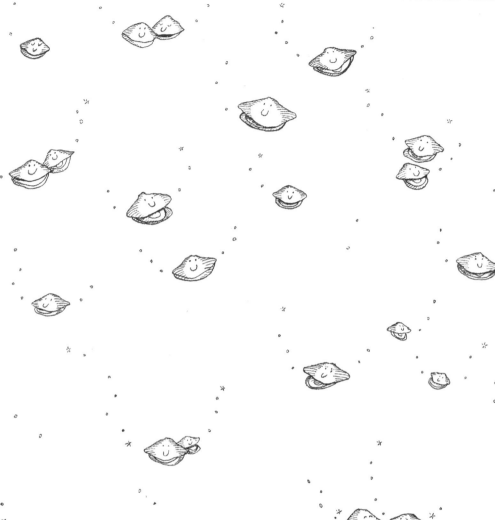

Kane/Miller Book Publishers, Inc.
First American Edition 2006
by Kane/Miller Book Publishers, Inc.
La Jolla, California

Copyright © 2005 by Naomi Kojima
First published in Japan in 2005 under the title "Utau Shijimi"
by Kaisei-Sha Publishing Co., Ltd.
English translation rights arranged with Kaisei-Sha Publishing Co., Ltd.
through Japan Foreign Rights Center

Library of Congress Control Number: 2006920863
Printed and bound in China
2 3 4 5 6 7 8 9 10

ISBN: 978-1-933605-12-8

Singing Shijimi Clams

By Naomi Kojima

Kane/Miller
BOOK PUBLISHERS

Once upon a time, there lived a witch.

When she was younger she was a mean and feisty witch, and she had liked nothing better than making fun of people and picking fights. But, now, perhaps because she was older, her sparks were gone, and she was simply miserable.

One day, the witch brought home some shijimi clams for her dinner.

She put the clams in a bowl with water to soak. She was preparing some bonito flakes for the broth when she heard a strange noise.

When she looked into the bowl, she saw that the clams were asleep and snoring. Their shells were opened slightly, and their little bodies moved contentedly.

The witch began to think it might be a bit cruel to eat the shijimi clams – after all, they were sleeping so peacefully. But her cat, Toraji, said, "They're just clams; we shouldn't feel sorry for them," and she agreed.

The broth began to boil, and the thought of miso soup made with shijimi clams was enough to make the witch's mouth water. But when she looked into the bowl, the clams were still sleeping, still snoring, and still moving contentedly.

"They won't feel anything if you put them in quickly," said Toraji.

"You're right! I must be going soft in my old age. Imagine, feeling sorry for a bunch of clams!" She poured the clams into a colander to drain.

They shut their shells quickly (and looked as if they might wake up), but settled themselves, and began to snore once more.

It was a little upsetting.

"Maybe we should eat the clams tomorrow night instead. There's nothing wrong with miso soup *without* shijimi clams, is there?" she asked Toraji.

Toraji looked away, fed up with the whole business.

The next evening, the witch began to make another pot of miso soup, but the shijimi clams were still sleeping peacefully...

"Don't even think about it," said Toraji, with a fierce (and hungry) look on his face.

"You're right, you're right," said the witch, chopping spring onions. "They're only clams."

But, just as she was about to pour them into the boiling broth...she stopped. She couldn't do it.

"Give them to me," snapped Toraji, "I'll do it!"

But once Toraji looked at the peaceful, sleeping clams, he couldn't do it either.

"What's the matter with us?" growled Toraji with frustration.

"Plain miso soup again tonight," replied the witch.

That night, as the witch lay in bed, she heard a noise. It sounded like lots of little voices, like lots of tiny popping bubbles.

Toraji came in to complain that the shijimi clams had woken him up.

When they went into the kitchen and looked into the bowl, they saw that the clams were wide awake and talking.

"I would like to ask you something, please..." The largest of the clams was speaking to the witch.

"Can you tell me where we are? Is this the sea? Is it a river?"

"It's my house," answered the witch, and all the shijimi clams burst into tears.

"They must have been taken away while they were sleeping," whispered Toraji. "That's why it's such a shock."

The clams wouldn't stop crying.

"Please don't cry, my dears," said the witch. "We will take you home."

"Wait," said Toraji in an urgent whisper. "That's easy to say, but how? How are we going to take them home?"

The witch used to be able to go everywhere on her broomstick, but it had become old and ragged and didn't work anymore.

"What about the train?" asked the witch.

"The train? There must be at least a hundred clams. How are we going to pay for the tickets?" Toraji was sounding exasperated.

It was true; the witch did not have much money.

"We should have eaten them the first night," said Toraji, and the clams cried harder.

"Don't cry, my dears," said the witch. "He's a kind cat really. Take no notice. We'll raise the money to get you home."

Toraji and the witch made a large sign, and stood on the street, ready to collect money for the shijimi clams.

They stood for hours.

They did not collect a single coin.

The witch was completely exhausted.

"Please don't be sad," cried the clams. "We'll sing for you."

And they began to sing with pretty little voices, like tiny popping bubbles.

People walking by stopped, and listened.

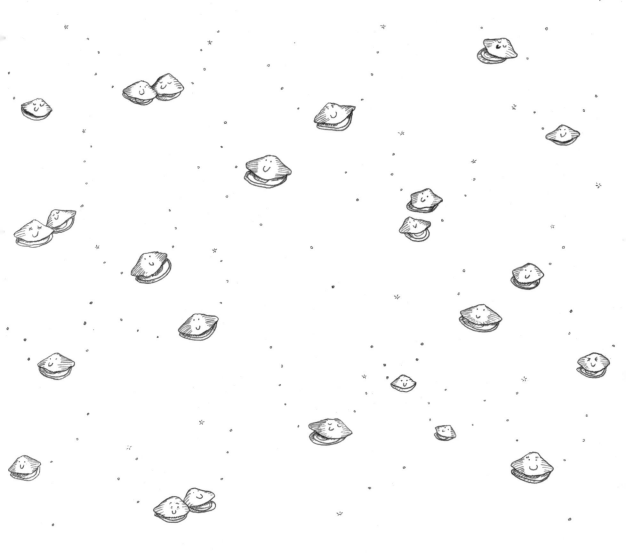

When they heard the shijimi clams singing, people forgot all their worries, their faces brightened, and a wonderful feeling came over them.

By the time it began to get dark, the shijimi clams had earned a lot of money.

Every day, as soon as the shijimi clams started to sing, people gathered and listened to their songs.

And every day, as the witch listened to the shijimi clams' sweet voices, she too began to feel happier, and less miserable.

Even Toraji seemed more content.

Then one evening, after about a month of singing and collecting, Toraji announced that they had enough money to buy all the train tickets.

The shijimi clams were so happy.

That night, while the witch lay in bed unable to sleep, Toraji snuck quietly into her room.

"I will miss them when they go," he admitted.

At the station the next morning, Toraji paid for the tickets, and they all got on the train.

The witch put the bowl by the window, so that the clams could see out too.

It was the first time that any of them – the witch, Toraji or the shijimi clams – had ever been on a train.

Before long, a wide expanse of sea, with a big river flowing into it, came into view.

When they arrived at the beach, the tide was out.

"Here we are," said the witch. She took the clams from the bowl and placed them on the sand. "The waves will soon come and take you home."

The shijimi clams gazed up silently.

They were too emotional to say "thank you" or "good bye."

The smallest clam finally said, "Miss Witch, Toraji, why don't you live here with us? Then we can sing for you every day."

"Yes, yes!" chorused the other clams.

The witch was quiet.

"What do you think?" she asked, turning to Toraji.

He was looking into his purse and frowning.

"Hmmm…"

He shook the empty purse and looked up at the witch with a worried expression.

"We forgot about return tickets," Toraji said. "We don't have any way to get home. I don't think we have a choice — we'll have to stay here."

"Hurrah!" shouted the clams.

And so, the witch and Toraji remained at the beach. They lived happily ever after, surrounded by the pretty voices of the clams, the gentle sound of the waves, and the warmth of the sun.